W9-APH-206

Quiz
Queens

K.L. Denman

Orca currents

ORCA BOOK PUBLISHERS

For Jessica Chase. She knows why.

Library and Archives Canada Cataloguing in Publication

Denman, K. L., 1957–, author
Quiz queens / K.L. Denman.
(Orca currents)

Issued in print and electronic formats.
ISBN 978-1-4598-1396-0 (paperback).—ISBN 978-1-4598-1397-7 (pdf).—
ISBN 978-1-4598-1399-1 (epub)

I. Title. II. Series: Orca currents
PS8607.E64Q59 2017   jC813'.6   C2016-904466-1
                            C2016-904467-X

First published in the United States, 2017
Library of Congress Control Number: 2016950078

Summary: In this high-interest novel for middle readers, boy-crazy Kiara
convinces studious Jane to create a questionnaire to help find her soulmate.

*Orca Book Publishers is dedicated to preserving the environment and has
printed this book on Forest Stewardship Council® certified paper.*

Orca Book Publishers gratefully acknowledges the support for its
publishing programs provided by the following agencies: the Government
of Canada through the Canada Book Fund and the Canada Council
for the Arts,and the Province of British Columbia through
the BC Arts Council and the Book Publishing Tax Credit.

Cover photography by Getty Images
Author photo by Jasmine Kovac

ORCA BOOK PUBLISHERS
www.orcabook.com

Printed and bound in Canada.

20 19 18 17 • 4 3 2 1

Chapter One

I have solid plans. Not just for today or tomorrow, but for the next ten years. My plans are going to take me places. And yet, here I am in the same old place, listening to Kiara. She's been my best friend since second grade, and she's great. She is. But lately I've started to wonder what we have in common.

We're doing what we usually do after school, hanging out in her room. She has spent the last twenty minutes talking about the utter cuteness of Omar Bari's eyes. She thinks they are so *deep*. Then she compares them to the amazing wonder of Liam Parks's biceps. Liam does have freakishly large biceps. I've told Kiara I don't have time to waste on guys. They only cause trouble. But does she listen? No. She is not a listener—she's a talker. Her parents regularly threaten her with duct tape. They've never actually taped her mouth shut, but they keep rolls of tape on hand.

My method to shut her up is to shut myself down. I stop making eye contact. I don't give her the smallest *Uh-huh*. It usually works. Like now, she finally flops onto her bed with her tablet. I sit at her desk, push my glasses into place (they're always sliding down my nose) and get started on my homework. Three whole minutes of silence pass.

"Omigod, Jane. Can you believe this?" Kiara taps the tablet screen. "It says my animal spirit totem is the coyote. As if."

"Another online personality quiz?" I ask.

"Yeah. And it's so wrong." She tosses back her ponytail. "I should have got the deer. At least they're pretty. Or the wolf. Wolves are cooler than coyotes."

I shake my head. "I don't know why you keep doing those things."

"Because they're fun."

"How are they fun?" I ask. "You hardly ever like the results."

Kiara looks surprised. "No way. Remember the fairy one I did yesterday? It said I was a flower fairy, and it described me perfectly. It said I'm sweet as nectar and love being around happy people. Totally accurate."

I sigh. "Yeah, but look what it took to get that. Three times doing the quiz and changing your answers until you got the fairy you wanted. Just like the dog one before that. You flipped when it said you were a golden retriever because you wanted to be a poodle. Or the Disney Princess one that said you're Cinderella and then Snow White before you got Jasmine."

Kiara shrugs. "So? You know how they work. It's multiple choice. Sometimes it's hard to decide which answer to pick. Let's say there's a picture of a grassy meadow, a beach and a full moon. I can't choose which one I like best if I like all of them."

"But," I argue, "aren't you supposed to go with your first instinct?" I can't believe I say that. I'm not big on following instincts.

"Yes." Kiara nods. "But it doesn't always work."

"Because," I say, "*they* don't work. They're garbage."

She frowns and smooths the cover on her bed. It's pale purple with big white flowers. "They aren't garbage. They help me get to know myself. It's like Ms. Kalkat says. Fourteen is an age when people are figuring out who they are."

Ms. Kalkat is our teacher for Career and Personal Planning class. We've been learning about personal growth. Thanks to Sherry, my mother—or *no* thanks to her—I feel done with personal growth already.

"So"—Kiara throws me a defiant look—"I'm going to do the spirit-totem quiz over, and I'll prove it."

"Have you even read what it says about the coyote spirit totem?" I ask.

"No."

I narrow my eyes. "Then how do you know it's wrong?"

"Fine. I'll read it." She picks up her tablet and starts reading aloud. "*Coyote spirit messages may appear as jokes to remind you not to take things too seriously.*"

"Hmm," I murmur. "What else?"

She keeps reading. "*Its ways are indirect, but the coyote is a teacher with a sense of humor and hidden wisdom. Coyote wisdom reveals the truth behind illusion. Don't be tricked by appearances.*" She snorts at this. "As if I would be."

"That actually sounds pretty cool."

"You think?" Kiara is doubtful. "I'd still feel better with a deer animal spirit. Deer are beautiful."

"I like the part about revealing the truth behind illusion." I should tell her why I like it. I'd like her to see that all the so-called truth in these quizzes is an illusion. But I'm tired of arguing about it.

"And look at this," Kiara says. *"Coyote wisdom often uses trickery to deliver its message.* That's interesting."

Coyote wisdom *is* interesting. Trickery to deliver a message? I've got to remember that. Maybe I could use it to cure Kiara's quiz craziness? In a way, trickery is what I've got planned for Sherry. "Did I tell you about the *real* quiz I found online?"

"*Real* quiz?" Kiara squints suspiciously. "You mean something boring like a math quiz?"

"No. Actually, it's not a quiz. It's a questionnaire."

She rolls her eyes.

"Let me explain. Sherry's boyfriend dumped her, like they all do. So she's a mess. Again. It doesn't make sense. She keeps falling for the same type of guy over and over. It's insane."

Kiara nods sympathetically. "Your mom is…" She doesn't finish her sentence, but I can fill in the blank. My mom is pathetic.

"So anyway," I continue, "I've given up trying to make her stop seeing guys. She says she can't. But I figured there had to be something I could do. So I looked online at some psychology stuff. And I found this questionnaire. It's supposed to help people get to know each other. I mean, *truly* know each other. They got some complete strangers to ask each other these questions, and guess what happened?"

"What?"

"Some of the strangers fell in love."

Kiara stares. "Like, *actual* love?"

I nod.

"Wow."

"I know, right? So I want to give it to Sherry. After she's had a few days to recover. If she agrees to try it with the next guy," I say, "who knows? Maybe she'll be able to screen out the losers before she falls for them."

"And find her true love?"

I frown. "I don't know about that. I'm hoping it stops the endless drama."

"Do you think she'll do it?" Kiara asks.

"Hard to know. But what about *you*? If you must do quizzes, why not do *professional* ones?" I definitely plan to be a professional. "There are lots of them online."

"Jane, you're a genius."

I grin. The cure was that easy? "I try."

Kiara sits up and leans toward me. "I'd like to see that questionnaire."

"Yeah? I printed it out. Just a sec." I reach into my pack and pull out my Sherry folder. I like to stay organized. Someone has to.

The questionnaire is a mere two pages, and Kiara takes it eagerly.

"This is it? It can't be too hard." She's smiling at the paper like she just met an actual flower fairy. "I could use this."

"For what?"

She reads out random questions. "*Would you like to be famous? What's your perfect day?* Ahh! *This* is perfect!"

A queasy ripple of worry spreads through my gut. "Kiara. What are you talking about?"

She glances at me, eyes shining. "I don't know if I'm ready to fall in *actual* love. But actual *like* would be good. But I can't decide between Omar and Liam. And I can't tell if they like me." She waves the questionnaire. "So if I could somehow get them to do this… "

Chapter Two

Kiara doesn't want to return the questionnaire. She only agrees after I give her the link to the site where I found it. Then I start packing up to leave.

"You aren't staying for supper?" she asks. "I want you to help me figure this out."

I open her bedroom door, and the aroma of her mom's famous chiles rellenos wafts in. I hesitate, but only for a moment. "I can't. I need to check on Sherry."

"Like how she checks on you?" Kiara scoffs. But then her eyes soften, and she shakes her head. "Sorry, Jane. I didn't mean that."

"It's okay," I lie. "See you tomorrow?"

"Yeah. But I'll call you later, right?"

Sherry is where I expect her to be. She is slumped on the couch in her pajamas, clutching a video-game controller. She's not playing the game. She's simply staring at the blank screen.

"Hey, Sherry," I say.

No reaction.

"Sherry? Mom?"

She stirs. "What?" Her eyes focus, and she looks at me. "Why are you here? Shouldn't you be at school?"

Wow. She's got it bad. "School ended three hours ago. It's suppertime."

She's only mildly surprised. She mutters something under her breath and waves a hand. "I'm not hungry."

I don't answer. I go into the kitchen and find some canned soup. I divide it between two bowls. While it heats in the microwave, I make toast and unwrap cheese slices. It's no chiles rellenos, but it'll do. When I bring a bowl to Sherry, she ignores it.

I return with the plate of toast and cheese and tell her, "He's not worth it. You know that."

She sighs and finally glances my way. I'm struck by how weary she looks. Without her makeup, Sherry is showing signs of age. Not that thirty-two is very old. But if this keeps up, she won't be able to tell men I'm her sister. Then again, the men she dates aren't all that smart.

"Eat something," I say. "You'll feel better."

She picks up a spoon. "I thought he was different."

"You always think that." I get my Sherry folder out of my pack and pull out the list I need. "You said that about Eddy, Darnell, Scott—"

"Jane." She cuts me off with a sour look. "Stop."

I shrug and give her a moment. That's all the encouragement she needs. "And he was so handsome," she continues. "He was *hot*."

"So is your soup," I say. "But if you don't hurry up and eat it, it won't be."

Obediently, she swallows a mouthful. "He even had a job."

"Yeah. And you do too. Which you skipped out on today."

Her gaze sharpens. "I called them."

Sherry works as a cashier in a super-market. She's taken a lot of broken-heart sick days. She reports having a migraine. Or that our toilet has exploded. Or she tells them I'm sick. I'm never sick. For work excuses, having a kid is convenient. "And were they okay about it?" I ask.

She shrugs. "I guess."

"Good."

I watch her finish her soup and toast, and then I gather the dishes. It's like this. When I turned twelve, Sherry made an announcement. She said that I was her equal. She put a good spin on it. She said I was more grown up than most adults she knew. This was probably true. She told me she knew I could handle it. To seal the deal, she asked me to stop calling her Mom. She said "Mom" made her sound like an authority figure. Equals don't need that.

What it really meant was that Sherry was tired of being my mother. She went on to confide that having a kid stopped guys from getting involved with her.

I was disappointed to know for sure that she was a cliché. As her equal, I told her that. She didn't like it and tried to ground me.

As her equal, I told her fine, she was grounded too. Since then, we've muddled along. She works, pays the bills and shops for groceries. I do most of the cooking— unless I'm eating at Kiara's—and the cleaning. I also make her return new shoes we can't afford even when she says they're for me. We wear the same size, but I would never wear the stuff *she* likes.

About five seconds after I've done the dishes, Kiara calls. I swear she has a sixth sense about my routine. "Hey," she says. "How's Sherry?"

"Better. She ate supper."

"That's a good sign. So did you give her the questionnaire?"

"Not yet," I reply. "She's not ready."

There's a pause before she asks, "Have you actually read it? The whole thing?"

"Yeah. Why?"

She sighs. "It's way complicated."

"What do you mean?"

"Okay, maybe for someone like you, it's fine. But it's got questions about death and being embarrassed and when did you last cry. How is that romantic? It's depressing."

"It's not depressing," I tell her. "It's *serious*. There's a difference."

"Yeah, I know. But how can I ask Omar and Liam stuff like that? Yuck."

It's nice to hear she's come to her senses. I don't say that to her. I say, "You're right. It's a bad idea."

"Well, not exactly. I mean, the *idea* is good. But it needs to be customized."

"Customized," I say. "What, like your dad's cars?" Her dad works at a high-end auto-body shop. He does amazing custom paintwork. I have never met my dad.

"Yes! That's it." Kiara sounds excited.

17

"You take some basic thing and make it better."

"Kiara. When I told you about this questionnaire, it wasn't to get you a boyfriend. It was about you giving up those dumb online quizzes. Or if you *have* to do them, then do quality ones. *Professional* ones."

"*Phffft*. You and the professionals. I'm telling you, Jane, this can work."

I have that queasy feeling in my gut again. "What exactly are you talking about?"

"We'll write our own quiz! You see? And really, you're almost a professional already. So it'll be good quality. Practically designer label."

I have to laugh. "Designer label, huh? Should we call it the Prada Quiz?"

She laughs too. "Okay, maybe not. But I really want you to help me. Will you?"

"Um…" I do *not* want to help her get a friggin' boyfriend.

"Pleeease? Come on, Jane. I already started. So far I've got, *What is your favorite color?* And, *What is your lucky number?*"

She does need help. At least some quality control.

"Pretty please?" she begs.

Maybe the right questions would make her see how difficult boyfriends are? "Fine."

Her delighted squeal hurts my ear. I can picture her jumping up and down. Sometimes that girl has way too much enthusiasm. She's on the school cheerleading squad. If the rest of them quit, she could handle it on her own.

"But," I caution, "we need to think about this. And try to use a scientific approach. Okay?"

She just squeals some more.

As usual, Kiara is getting her way.

Chapter Three

The assignments in Career and Personal Planning class are easy. Today is no exception. *Create a Personal Timeline.* I could do that in my sleep. (1) Get perfect grades and graduate high school. (2) Win full scholarships for university. (3) Get a degree in business management for a secure job future. (4) Launch a career that provides respect and a big salary so that I will not end up like my mother.

I'm finished long before the bell will ring. I look at Kiara at the desk beside me. She's frowning over the assignment. I'd help her, but Ms. Kalkat passes out detentions like pigeons pass poop. Talk during work time is forbidden. Thanks to Kiara, we've had more than our share of poop.

I decide to use this time to consider Kiara's quiz. She wants to ask questions that will help her get to know Omar and Liam. My nose wrinkles. Such a lame goal. And what about them? Will they even go along with it? Will they laugh at her? I'd hate to see her get hurt.

They're both in our class, so it's possible to observe them. I've been sucked into this, so I might as well do my best. Luckily, both of them are seated at desks to my right. A slight adjustment to my angle is all I need to discreetly check them out.

Omar does have beautiful eyes. Big, deep brown, thickly lashed. He is using them to ogle Lexi Taylor. She's sitting directly in front of him, wearing her favorite leopard-print tights. The tights are strained to their limit, keeping that butt contained. Omar seems mesmerized. I am bored.

At first glance, Liam appears to be working on the assignment. However, closer study reveals this may not be the case. He's holding his pen in his left hand, but he isn't writing with it. No, he's doing some sort of exercise. The muscles in his arm are twitching. Okay, they are not exactly twitching. The correct word would be *flexing*. This is interesting. I pick up my pen and clench it. The muscles in my forearm move—a tiny bit. Not nearly enough for anyone else to notice. There's something fascinating about Liam's rippling muscles. It's as if they have an independent life. That's a foolish thought. I look past Liam to see if other nearby males have this ability. I notice the new kid, Javier. He's hunched over his papers and is mostly invisible. His wild, curly hair hides most of his face, and his plaid shirt covers his arms. The only muscle movement I can see is his hand, working the pen. Very ordinary.

Back to Liam. He's amped things up. He's crumpled his work sheet into a ball and laid his forearm on his desktop, his hand palm up. He squeezes the paper ball, and his bicep muscles bulge. The underarm seam on his black T-shirt is ripped open. Is this why muscled people are said to be "ripped"? I suddenly have a strange impulse to reach out and stroke his arm. Why would I think that?

And then Liam looks straight at me and grins. Like he knows I wanted to touch him. My face flames, and I turn away—fast. I think I hear him chuckle. I also think that grin reminds me of someone. Who? And then I know. Sherry's losers. They all have that grin.

I want to tell Kiara I've changed my mind. Guys are way too dangerous. But she practically dances the whole way home from school and doesn't shut up long enough for me to say a word.

I decide I'll tell her when we're back in her room. After she hands me a bag of my favorite pecan cookies, I can't do it. "I asked Mom to make them especially for you," she says.

"Kiara..."

"No, no, Jane. You deserve them. Don't worry—she made lots. Plenty for everyone."

"That's good." My smile is weak. "I wouldn't want another raid from the twins." Kiara has seven-year-old twin brothers. They're terrors, and I love them like they are my own brothers.

"Okay!" Kiara claps her hands. "Let's do this."

I stop myself from rolling my eyes and settle for a sigh. "Are you *sure* about this?"

"Totally. Why?"

"No reason." It occurs to me that it's one thing to make a list of questions. But in typical Kiara style, her plan is incomplete. She hasn't thought about how she'll get Omar and Liam to participate. This scheme is doomed, so there is no need for me to talk her out of it. "What have you got so far?"

"Um…I told you already. Favorite color and lucky number."

"Huh. Okay." I reach into my pack and pull out a pen and paper. "Why are those questions important?"

She looks at me with something like pity. "Isn't it obvious? If I know his favorite color, I can wear it. And if I know his lucky number, I can pick that date to make my move."

"Your move?"

She giggles. "You know. Like, if his lucky number is five? Then on the fifth of next month, I'll…flirt with him."

I raise my brows. "Seriously? Do you even know *how* to flirt?"

"For sure. I've watched some online tutorials. It's easy. You have to make eye contact and have the right posture." She must see something in my face because she adds, "I mean, body language. Like, don't cross your arms."

"Omigod," I mutter under my breath. "It's worse than I thought."

"What?"

"Nothing. What if his lucky number is something like forty-three?"

"It won't be. Jeez, Jane. Who would have that?"

I shrug. "I don't know. It's possible."

"Well, if he's *that* weird I won't be interested. Can we just start making more questions?"

I pick up my pen. "How about this one? *If you ever become famous, what would you like to be famous for?*"

She tips her head to one side and considers. "Yeah. I like it."

I scribble down the question. "All right. Here's another one. *Have you ever cheated on anything or anyone?*"

"Hmm. Why would I ask that?"

"Because it's important. Remember Sherry's boyfriends? Numbers two, four and seven?"

Her eyes widen. "Right. She was really hurt. So yeah. We'll include it. And maybe we should have a question about honesty too. Like, *How important is honesty in a relationship?*"

"Good one." I jot down both questions. "I think we could use the one you liked from the questionnaire. Something to do with your perfect day?"

"Yeah. *Describe your perfect day.* Then maybe another easy one like, *What is your favorite movie?*"

"That's a little *too* easy. How about *which is more important, beauty or brains?* And *why?*"

"Nice." Kiara nods.

My pen moves again. "Okay, we've got seven so far. If we get three more, we'll have ten. That should be enough."

A few minutes pass while we ponder. Kiara comes up with, "*What is your favorite plant?*"

I look at her. "Um…why?"

She shrugs. "I don't know. I'm running out of ideas."

"I believe you. How about asking if they like kids? That tells you something about a person."

"True." She nods. "But the kid one is risky. They might think it means I'm crazy. Like I'm already looking to get married. Or even that I'm pregnant and…" She stops and bites her lip. "Sorry, Jane. I wasn't thinking."

"No worries. You have a point. Don't want to scare them off with a kid." I take off my glasses to clean them while I think. "Maybe the question could be *do you like pets?* Or, *What's your favorite animal?*"

"Yeah!" She nods vigorously. "Favorite animal. Good one."

I write it down. "Two more. Ah! How about asking, *What superpower would you like to have?*"

"Oooh. Yes!"

"One more. And I think I've got a good one. *What are your plans for the future?*"

Kiara frowns. "I don't know. That's a boring question."

I point my pen at her. "But it's important."

She rolls her eyes. "When you're fourteen?"

"*Especially* when you're fourteen." I add the question to our list. "There. That's ten. We're done. Do you want me to type it up on the computer?"

"That would be great. And then…" She hesitates. This is when her plan fizzles and dies.

"And then?" I prompt. I could be smirking.

Gleefully she hugs me. "I've got it all figured out, Jane. You won't believe it."

Chapter Four

Kiara is right. I don't believe she's got this figured out. I take a pecan cookie from the bag and lean back in my chair. "Okay. So tell me."

She moves to sit cross-legged on her bed and composes herself. She presses her hands together under her chin like she's praying.

"You're going to do yoga?" I ask.

She laughs. "No." But she takes a deep yoga-type breath before giving me a sideways look. "You might not like it."

"Why not?"

"Because it's sort of tricky. Like the coyote."

I have a bad feeling about this. "Just tell me already."

"Okay. So what I want to do is make two copies of the quiz. One for Omar and one for Liam. Then we'll put them in an envelope with a letter that says this is a chance to earn extra marks. For Career and Personal Planning."

"I don't get it."

"Wait. There's more." Her eyes are huge. "Then we'll sneak the envelopes onto their desks."

"Ummm…"

Kiara holds up a hand. "And obviously, we don't want them to give these back to Ms. Kalkat."

"Obviously."

"So the letter will instruct them each to hand in the completed quiz at the office. To Mrs. Peebles."

Mrs. Peebles is the ancient office secretary. She's often confused. Sometimes she forgets to turn off the school PA system, and we hear her singing. It's always the same song. "*Old MacDonald had a farm. E-I-E-I-O…*" Personally, I think she's trying to tell us something.

"And how do you get the quizzes back from Mrs. Peebles?" I ask. I'm pretending to go along with this plan. But the more I hear, the more I hate it.

"Glad you asked. Mrs. Peebles likes you, Jane."

It's true. I was in the office one time when she broke into song. I sang along with her. "So?"

"So I was thinking. You could go to her. Tell her you're doing an extra project. She'll believe it because you're an overachiever. You could tell her it's an anonymous survey to see how many people will complete an anonymous survey."

I glare at Kiara. "You want me to lie to Mrs. Peebles?"

She rolls her eyes. "It won't hurt her or anything. All you have to do is go back later and ask her for them. And, voilà!" She watches me eagerly. Like she thinks I'm going to be impressed.

I take a bite of my cookie and try to decide where to start. "So. Let me get this straight. You want to trick the guys into doing the quiz. Then you want me to trick Mrs. P. And nowhere in this so-called plan do I see *you* doing the quiz. With them."

Her nose wrinkles. "I can't do *that*."

"Wasn't that the whole point? You do the quiz with them. So you get to know each other?"

She waves her hands. "No, no, no! That's only for that professional thing *you* have. For Sherry. There's no way I can get up the nerve to ask them. But I want to see what *they're* like."

I pick up the list of questions we wrote. I feel like tearing it up. One question in particular stands out. I read it aloud. *"How important is honesty in a relationship?"*

Kiara blinks. "What?"

"This question. You wanted it on the list. So I'm asking you. How would you answer that one, Kiara?"

She turns pink. "Jane. It's only a quiz. I'm not hurting anyone."

"But you obviously expect *them* to think honesty is important. And me too. And you're asking me to *lie* for you? You know I won't do that." It's true. With Sherry, I've seen how much damage lies can cause.

She looks away. Her chin is trembling. "Jane, come on. You're taking this too seriously. And how often do I ask you for a favor? Hardly ever."

"No?" I scoff. "You asked me to help you with this quiz."

Her chin goes up. "Yeah. And you said you would. Now you want to go back on your word?"

I open my mouth to tell her that was before I found out I had to lie. But I snap my mouth shut as I get an idea. A coyote idea. One that might fix this whole thing. My idea would mean no boyfriend troubles for Kiara. And it would teach her a lesson about honesty. It's about time I stood up for myself.

I fold the sheet of questions and slide it into my pack. "Fine. I'll *help* you. I'll take this home and get it ready tonight."

She squeals and leaps off the bed. "Yes! Thank you!" She wraps me in a hug. "Omigod, this is sooo exciting."

She bounces up and down. "You're the best bestie ever, Jane."

I have to agree. Friends don't let friends be fools.

Chapter Five

When I get home, Sherry is much better. She's wearing clothes and is actively playing her video game. She's not up to asking about my day. That is just as well. I would have to tell her it sucked.

After our gourmet meal of salad and grilled cheese sandwiches, I get Sherry to promise she'll go back to work tomorrow. Then *I* get to work. This is the letter I write to go with the quiz:

Dear Student,

Enclosed is a quiz. You are receiving this optional work to provide you with an opportunity to earn extra marks. Return your completed quiz, sealed in this envelope, to Mrs. Peebles, the office secretary.

Do <u>not</u> write your name on your quiz. Due to the nature of the questions, your identity is protected. Each quiz is numbered. Your number has been recorded. If your quiz is returned, the number on it will be matched to your name for credit, but answers will be kept anonymous.

Good luck.
The Career and Personal Planning Team

I couldn't bring myself to forge Ms. Kalkat's name. But I'm okay with saying I'm part of "The Career and Personal Planning Team." Kiara might be my only student, but I *am* helping her with personal planning.

Next, I type up the quiz questions. I make nice blank lines for the answers. It looks good. Professional. Too easy? Hmm. I toy with the idea of adding more questions. If the school was getting us to answer an anonymous questionnaire, it wouldn't be like this one. It would have questions about drugs, alcohol, home life and sex. We're asked to do those sometimes, so they know how many of us are "at risk."

But the offer of extra marks should be enough to motivate the guys. I'm pretty sure they need all the help they can get. I have to give Kiara credit for that idea. Then I print out three copies of the quiz. I carefully pencil a random number on the upper right-hand corner of each: 17, 22, 5. I print three copies of the letter and put one and a quiz into each envelope.

I double-check the rotating class schedule. Career and Personal Planning is first period tomorrow. I take a shower, do my homework, then go to check on Sherry.

"I'll get up early with you tomorrow," I tell her.

"You don't have to," she says. "I'll be fine."

"I need to get to school early anyway."

"Suit yourself." She yawns. Then she looks at me. "But thanks, Jane."

She can be all right sometimes.

The last thing I do before bed is check my phone. I kept it off all evening. There are ten missed calls, all from Kiara. And about ten more text messages. I send a reply. **Hey. No worries. The quiz is ready. I'm going to**

bed early. Have to make sure Sherry gets up for work. See you at school!

Then I turn my phone off again. And I leave it off the next morning. As promised, I make sure Sherry gets up and out the door for work. Then I gather up the envelopes and my books and head for school.

Mrs. Peebles is pleased to see me. "Jane, dear. You're here early. Is everything okay?"

"Just fine, Mrs. P. I came to ask a favor."

"If I can do it," she says, beaming, "I will."

I feel terrible about lying to her. I choose my words carefully so they're not totally dishonest. I show her one of the envelopes. "I'm going to be handing these out to some students. It's for an extracurricular project. But it's anonymous. So I'm hoping the students will return them to you. And then I'll stop by later to pick them up."

"Ah." She nods. "I'll bet you're too shy to let them see how smart you are. Tsk-tsk. I hope you get past that one day, Jane. Do you remember what Dolly Parton said?"

"Um…no." I've heard the name Dolly Parton, but I have no idea who this is.

"She said, *Find out who you are and do it on purpose.* Isn't that great advice?"

"Yes." I nod earnestly. "That's really good." It actually is. I'd like to think I'm following it right now. "So." I waggle the envelope. "Is this okay with you?"

"Absolutely, dear."

"Thanks, Mrs. P. See you later."

She waves me off, and I head for Career and Personal Planning. As I hoped, no one else is there yet. I set my pack on my desk and prepare to distribute the envelopes.

Then Ms. Kalkat walks in. "Jane. You're here early."

Does everyone have to state the obvious? "Yes."

"Is everything all right?"

And everyone has to ask me that? "All good," I reply.

"Excellent. Then I wonder if I might ask you a favor?" She's holding a stack of paper. "Would you mind putting these out on everyone's desk for me?"

My grin feels huge. "No problem, Ms. Kalkat. I'd be happy to."

"Thank you. I forgot something in the staff room. I'll be right back."

"Okay." I take the stack of paper, our assignment for today. I work fast, laying one on each desk. When I reach Omar's and Liam's desks, it's easy to slide their envelopes under the assignment. But who should get the third quiz?

I haven't decided, but it doesn't really matter. Javier? Why not? I don't bother to check which number they get. That won't matter either.

Chapter Six

I'm laying the last assignment paper on the last desk when someone hisses, "*Jane!*" I spin to find Kiara advancing on me. "What are you doing?"

I smile. "What does it look like? Ms. Kalkat asked me to hand these out."

Still whispering, she asks, "What about the quizzes?"

My smile widens. "All done." I gesture toward the assignment papers. "Perfect cover, eh?"

She brings a hand to her mouth. "No way. Are you kidding me?" She wraps me in a hug. "How did you manage that?"

"I didn't have to do anything. Ms. Kalkat just showed up and"—I shrug—"it happened."

"Wow. It's like an omen."

"What?"

Her eyes are huge. "An omen. That this is the right thing to do. I mean, to have it work out so easily—it's practically a miracle."

"A miracle? I don't know if I'd go that far."

She grips my arm. "Maybe not. But it's definitely a good sign." She tugs me toward Omar's and Liam's desks. Her eyes fixate on their assignment papers. "So." She points. "The envelopes are there?"

I nod.

"Ooooh." She bounces a bit. "What about the letter?"

"The letter?"

"I want to see the letter you wrote."

"Um…" I stall. "I don't have an extra copy with me."

"But I want to see it!" She eyes the paper on Omar's desk. The edge of the envelope tucked underneath is visible. There is no way I want her to see that letter. Kiara makes a move toward Omar's desk, and I block the way.

"Are you nuts?" I ask.

"What?"

"We don't want to be caught messing around with that. I say we get out of here and come back when the bell rings."

She glances nervously at the door. "You could be right."

"I am. Let's go." I stride toward the door. A second later, I'm relieved to hear her footsteps following. As we walk out, Ms. Kalkat returns.

The moment we're past her, Kiara breathes, "You were right, Jane. Phew." Then she bounces some more and adds, "I'm so nervous."

"Relax," I tell her.

But she doesn't. She lurks in the hall near the door, watching the other kids file in. When Javier passes by, she whispers, "That guy needs help."

She could be right. Javier is tall and skinny, and he moves like a drunken giraffe. It's as if his limbs don't want to go in the same direction. He also has a peculiar way of bobbing his head sometimes. It's unclear if he's nodding hello or trying to duck and hide. I have a momentary pang of guilt over giving him a quiz. It could be confusing for him. But it's too late now.

The moment Omar and Liam are through the door, so is Kiara. Once seated, she remains hyperaware of them. She notices when they discover their envelopes. She squeaks when she sees the guys exchange frowns over their quizzes. And she gurgles loudly (a suppressed shriek) when Liam picks up his pen.

"Kiara?" Ms. Kalkat calls. "Are you all right?"

"I'm fine." Kiara flushes deep pink.

"Then would you kindly focus on your work? *Quietly*. Or would you rather do that at the end of the day?" The threat of poop is real.

Kiara shakes her head and turns over her paper. Today's assignment is to identify the steps in the decision-making process. We've done this before. Maybe the timelines we did yesterday revealed students with poor decision-making skills? So Ms. Kalkat decided we needed a review?

Whatever. I like the decision-making process. It's comforting to see all those logical steps. If more people followed the steps, there wouldn't be so many bad decisions out there. The first time we got a work sheet on this, I showed it to Sherry and told her it would help prevent impulsive, emotional choices. She barely glanced at it. She said her feelings were too powerful to be tamed by some snotty process.

I finish the assignment and glance over at Kiara. She looks strange. Like maybe she had a seizure. Her head is tilted over her left shoulder, and one eye is fixed on the paperwork. The other eye is aimed in a different direction. Okay, it's just an illusion caused by her lightning-fast shifts in focus. Paper. Boys. Paper. Boys. Impressive.

Ms. Kalkat tells us that anyone who hasn't finished can complete the assignment for homework. It's time for a class discussion on planning. Her discussions are usually more like lectures, and today is no exception. She repeats her favorite Benjamin Franklin quote on the topic. "*If you fail to plan, you are planning to fail.*"

Kiara shoots me a triumphant look. I know what she's thinking. She made a plan, and it didn't fail. As soon as the bell rings, she leans over and says, "They did it! I saw them!"

"Cool," I reply.

"Did the letter say to hand the quizzes back to Mrs. P.?" she asks.

"Of course."

"Okay. Good." She claps her hands. "Do you think they'll take it there right away?"

"Probably not. We've barely got time to get to our next class."

She chews on her lip. "Yeah. So maybe at lunchtime."

"Maybe." I sigh. "But don't they usually hang out with their friends in the cafeteria? Why don't we wait until after school?"

"But I've got cheerleading practice then!"

I pat her arm. "Don't worry. I'll go get them from Mrs. P., and then I'll wait for you. Okay?"

"Okay." She doesn't look like it's okay. She looks like she might have a meltdown. But I'm keeping control of this situation, and she will have to wait.

Somehow we make it through the day. There's an awkward moment at lunch. Kiara insists on staking out the office. We see plenty of students come and go, including Omar. And Javier.

"Omigod," Kiara squeals. "Go get it."

"No. Liam hasn't returned his, and I don't want to bug Mrs. P. more than I have to."

"She won't mind!"

The warning bell sounds. "She might. And now we don't have time anyway.

Just chill for a couple more hours, Kiara. I'll meet you after practice."

It's very important that I get to the quizzes before Kiara has a chance to see them.

Chapter Seven

It works out exactly as I had hoped. Almost. I don't expect to bump into Liam as he's leaving the office. Literally. He's staring at the phone in his hand as he rounds the corner, and boom. Full collision. He reaches out and grabs my arm to steady me.

"Whoops. Sorry, uh…" He doesn't remember my name.

"Jane," I mutter. He's still holding my arm, and the contact is…stunning.

"Right. Jane." He grins that grin. *That* one. And then he releases me. "You okay?"

I nod. I can't trust my voice.

"Cool. Later." And he's gone.

I rub my tingling arm. I think maybe I should rub my knees too, because they're wobbling. Bizarre. And then I get it. Some traitorous part of me is attracted to him. How icky is that? How is it possible? Did I inherit a serious flaw from Sherry? Maybe there's a gene that makes a person like swaggering bad boys?

But before I can analyze my reaction, Mrs. P. spots me. "Jane. There you are." She picks up the familiar envelopes and waves them. "You've got some responses here."

"Great," I croak. I clear my throat and move to take them. "Thanks."

"Good luck with your results," she trills.

"Thanks again, Mrs. P. For everything. Really." I head for the library. I find a private spot and tear open the envelopes. The first quiz is almost blank. The favorite-color question is answered with *Blue*. And then, scrawled into the space for favorite animal, is the word *Me*.

"Yeesh," I mutter. "Probably Liam." But, as instructed, he didn't put his name on it. I put the quiz into a fresh envelope and seal it.

The next quiz is fully completed. Wow. I don't take time to read it. I check to make sure there is no name on it, and then I seal it in a new envelope. I repeat this process with the third quiz, which is partially completed. It also contains the cover letter I wrote. I shove that into my pack. There. Now I can hand them over to Kiara and…

And she'll learn an important lesson. I'm not kidding myself. I know she'll be angry. At first. But once she sees my point, she should be fine. She might even thank me.

I refuse to let Kiara open the envelopes until we're in her room with the door closed. Her hands are shaking when she finally gets hold of them.

"I can't breathe," she says.

"Just open them already."

"Wait." She blinks in confusion. "Why are there three of them?"

"You'll see," I tell her.

"But…" She gives me a piercing look. "Jane. What did you do?"

"Are you going to open them or what?"

That gets her. She tears open the first one and scans it. "Favorite color is blue. And oooh! He'd like to have invisibility for a superpower."

"That's a bit creepy."

She's not listening. She's frowning at the quiz. "But who wrote this? There's no name on it!" She flips the paper over and checks the back. "No name," she repeats. "*Jane*." Her voice is high with panic. "You forgot to put a place for them to write their name."

"Um…" I push my glasses into place. "I didn't exactly forget."

"What?"

"I thought they'd be more likely to do it if it was anonymous. So I just put numbers on them."

"Oh. So who got this one? It's number five."

"I don't know."

Her eyes bulge. "You didn't keep track of their numbers?"

I could lie. I could tell her I messed up on the numbers. But I won't do that. "No, I didn't track them. I thought it would be more fun for you to figure out who wrote what."

Her lower lip is trembling. "But what if I *can't*?"

I shrug. "I'll bet you can."

"I don't know. This wasn't what I planned, and you…" She stops and gives me a hard look. Her jaw tightens as she finishes reading over the first quiz. Without a word, she folds it and sets it aside.

She opens the next one. I can see it's the one I suspect Liam returned. Kiara is done with it quickly and sets it aside. Her hand is shaking worse than ever as she opens the third and reads. And reads. Finally, she speaks. "Wow. This is just—wow."

"Can I see?" I ask.

She looks at me suspiciously. "Why? It almost looks like something you'd write."

This is insulting. "No way," I scoff. "Believe me, I didn't write it."

"Then who did? Who is the third guy, Jane? Is it even a guy?"

"It's a guy. But I'm not going to tell you who."

"What?" She glares at me. "Why not?"

I raise my hands, palms up. "Because it doesn't matter."

Her mouth falls open. She looks dazed as she murmurs, "It doesn't matter?" Then she shakes her head. "How can you say that? You *have* to tell me!"

I probably should tell her it was Javier. But for once, I feel like the one with the power. It feels surprisingly good. And scary and slimy all at the same time. I want to keep it at least long enough to figure it out. Besides, giving her what she wants won't prove my point. Which is that you can't truly like someone you don't know.

"Not yet. Maybe later. I'm trying to help you figure this out."

"No, you're not. All you've done is screw it up. And now I don't have a clue which guy wrote what. It's impossible!"

"Nothing is impossible." I decide to stall her. "Let me see them." I hold out my hand. After a moment she reluctantly passes a quiz to me. It's the one with *me* for favorite animal. "Okay. Think about it. Which guy is most likely to call himself an animal?"

"I don't know. It's obviously a joke."

"Either that," I say, "or he's really into himself." I hold up an arm and flex my bicep.

She doesn't pick up on my hint. This is unlike her. Normally, she'd be happy to talk about which guy might be conceited enough to be his own favorite animal. Instead she says, "The only other thing on it is favorite color blue. Which they *all* say."

"Really? So no clues from color. Huh. Imagine that. Let me see another one." She hands me the one with the invisibility superpower. It says *Dog* for favorite animal. And *Not really* to the question about cheating. A perfect day is *Sleep in, hang out with friends and eat pizza.*

"See?" Kiara says. "That could be anyone."

She's right. I could make my point now, but instead I ask to see the third quiz. She looks like she might refuse, but then she tosses it over. I find this:

1. What is your favorite color? _Blue_

2. What is your lucky number? _3_

3. If you ever become famous, what would you like to be famous for? _I'd like to be famous for bringing about world peace. Also, possibly for the invention of a time machine._

4. Have you ever cheated on anything or anyone? _No_

5. How important is honesty in a relationship? _It is very important. Without honesty, there is no trust._

6. Describe your perfect day. _Take a jet to Africa and go on safari. Meet unusual people. Feast with family and friends. Sleep under the stars._

7. Which is more important, beauty or brains? _Beauty_ Why? _Because true beauty is on the inside and being smart doesn't make a person good._

8. What's your favorite animal? _Wolf_

9. What superpower would you like to have? _Flight_

10. What are your plans for the future? _I plan to follow my curiosity._

Wow. I never expected anything like this. I look up to find Kiara glaring again. She's also winding the end of her ponytail around and around her finger. She only does that when she's tense. "Um...this one is really interesting. Who do you think wrote it?" I ask.

"How should I know? Since you're so clever, why don't *you* tell *me*?"

"No idea. I've never talked to any of them."

She makes a weird little sound in her throat, like a muffled scream. When she speaks, her voice oozes sarcasm. "So that's all you've got, Jane? *Nothing*?"

"Who do you want it to be?" I ask.

"I don't know. Maybe Omar? But thanks to *you*, I can't be sure. All I know is, whoever it is, *he* would be the one."

"The *one*?"

"Don't mock me, Jane. You've put me in a terrible predicament."

"I think you put yourself there," I reply.

"Oh, really? And how did I do that?"

I'll have to explain it to her. "Okay. You said you like Omar and Liam. But how is that even possible? You don't know them at all. You know nothing about who they *are* as people. Which is exactly how Sherry operates. And look where that got her."

"I'm not Sherry! And I was *trying* to get to know them." She shakes one of the quizzes at me. "With *this*."

"But you went about it dishonestly. By trickery. I mean, again, look at this question about the importance of honesty." I point to the fully answered quiz. "Whoever wrote this answer gets it. Without honesty in a relationship, there is no trust."

"You know who doesn't get that, Jane?" she hisses. "You! You don't get it. *You* deceived *me*. So I don't trust you anymore. You see?" She looks like she might cry. "I think you should go."

"Kiara—"

"No. I mean it, Jane. We're done." She snatches the quiz from me and points at her bedroom door. "Leave. Now."

She looks serious.

I try again. "But—"

"No buts! Get out of here. I'm sick of you and your superior attitude. The only reason I stayed friends with you so long is I felt sorry for you. Get out."

Chapter Eight

She feels sorry for me? I'm too stunned to even ask what she means. My entire body feels numb as I grab my bag and fling myself out the door. By the time I'm home, being stunned has worn off. It's been replaced by near-total confusion. All I know is, she'll call. She will. She'll call and apologize. I'll ask what she meant about feeling sorry for me.

And I'll get a chance to explain that I was trying to protect her.

I wait all evening, and she doesn't call. I finally go to bed but don't sleep well. I have disturbing dreams that I can't remember, even when they wake me. When my alarm goes off in the morning, I'm groggy. The first thing I reach for is my phone. There are zero missed calls. No text messages.

Wow. Kiara and I have had squabbles before, but none ever led to her kicking me out of her room. Nor did they last this long. This is bad. I toy with the idea of sending her a text. But what would I say? I could say I'm sorry, but for what? Trying to be her true friend? Which is what I am. A friend trying to save her from trouble.

Maybe she needs more examples of how crappy boyfriends can be. Obviously, I've told her all about Sherry's troubles. But what if she thinks that's only a Sherry problem? Kiara has a fairly charmed life. She probably believes she's immune to mayhem of the heart.

I'm not immune. I can't believe she said that about staying friends because she felt sorry for me.

No, I'm not going to apologize. I need to stand by what I did until she figures it out. She can be stubborn, but so can I. She's used to getting her way, and now that I've done what *I* think is right, I need to stick with it.

I check my phone again, and there's nothing.

She avoids me at school. I glimpse her in the hall at lunchtime, walking with a group of cheerleaders. Career and Personal Planning is last period today, so I bide my time until then. Once we're sitting right beside each other, she'll cave. I know she will.

But she doesn't show up for class. Unbelievable. I risk detention poop by sending her a text: **Where are you?**

I don't get a reply. I do get the poop. Ms. Kalkat confiscates my phone and doesn't return it until I've passed a dazed half hour after school. I trudge home to our empty apartment. It's dingy, and the air smells stale. There's also a lingering whiff of Sherry's cheap perfume. No warm scent of pecan cookies baking. I open a window and consider making something nice for supper. Meatloaf? Chicken pot pie? Chiles rellenos?

Who am I kidding? I don't know how to cook those things. And the chances of us having the ingredients are slim. A check in the cupboards confirms this. Canned spaghetti will have to do.

I could catch up on cleaning. I wander into the bathroom, and yes, there are long Sherry hairs everywhere. She has been dying her hair auburn for years. The last time she did it, her hair turned out more orange than auburn. I look at my own hair in the mirror. It's an ordinary shade of brown, the color Sherry's would be if she didn't dye it. I usually wear mine in a braid so I don't have to waste time on it. I experiment with changing the part to the other side—until I realize I'm doing a Sherry thing, and that's just wrong.

I'm bored. Maybe I could get a cat. A black one. Or one of those striped tabby cats. Possibly a calico. Pets aren't allowed in our building, but I decide to look up cats online. Instead I find myself signing into social media. I rarely bother with it (another time waster—so many cat videos), but I have time today. I can also check who else is online. And what their status is.

Kiara has blocked me. How immature is that? I block her too, then immediately unblock her. I refuse to stoop to that level. Instead I read a post by my second-favorite scientist, Neil deGrasse Tyson. My number-one favorite is Jane Goodall. Tyson is writing about how Batman can beat Superman. Hmm. Then I find his list of the eight books every intelligent person on the planet should read. I review the list and find I have a lot of reading to do.

My phone buzzes with a text message. I lunge for it and find a message from Sherry. **Hey, something has come up. I'll be home late. Go ahead and stay at Kiara's for supper. xo**

I groan aloud. Another guy already? It must be. When Sherry says *something has come up*, it's her code for a date. She probably thinks I don't know that, but I do. I swear she must have a sign on her cash register. The sign says, *Single and desperate*. Or *I date losers*. Or maybe *Take me out on trial*.

Whatever. I don't bother to reply. I eat the spaghetti straight out of the can and try to do my homework. For the first time ever, I have trouble staying focused.

Chapter Nine

The next day is no better. Kiara shows up for Career and Personal Planning class, but it's like there's a wall of ice around her. Every time I glance her way, she's either staring straight ahead or down at her work. I know she must sense my gaze, but she gives no sign. Not the flicker of an eye. Not a hunched shoulder or thinned lips. She does spend a moment twisting the end of her pony-tail. But that only happens when Omar passes by her desk.

It's like I've ceased to exist. I spend lunch in the library and go straight home again after school. Friday is the same, and then it's Friday night. I've slept over at Kiara's nearly every Friday since sixth grade. We watch movies. Sometimes we babysit her brothers. (They try to prank us, every time. We pretend to be fooled, every time.) We listen to music and eat popcorn and talk. We talk about every-thing and everyone.

I'm alone on the couch in our apart-ment, remembering past conversations. *Which is better, caramel or chocolate? Is there life on other planets? Why did Lexi Taylor's butt get so big? Should Kiara paint her desk yellow or mauve? Is there life after death?* I don't notice I'm crying until Sherry bursts in. She's laughing. She also has a guy with her.

"Jane?" Sherry gapes at me like she's never seen me before. "What are you doing here?"

I swipe my sleeve across my face and retort, "I live here. Remember?"

"But...it's Friday. Shouldn't you be at Kiara's?"

"Who's that?" I ask dully.

There's silence. Then Sherry turns to the guy and says, "Sorry, Clive. Change of plans. We'll have to go somewhere else."

"Why?" He's a skinny guy with slicked-back hair. His voice is surly. "Can't you just tell your kid to go to her room or somethin'?"

"She's not my—" Sherry stops and looks at me. Then she turns to him. Her eyes are cold as she says, "No. I can't."

"What? You kiddin' me?" Clive is shaking his head. "What kind of mother are you? Just tell the kid to scram."

Sherry moves toward the door.

"That's the problem with parents these days." Clive wags a finger at Sherry. "No discipline skills. Lettin' your kids run your life."

Sherry opens the door. "Goodbye, Clive."

He stares at her, disbelieving. "You ain't comin'?"

My stare is equally shocked.

"Nope," Sherry says. "I *ain't*."

He steps through the door. "Fine. But I'm warnin' you. You do this, and we're done."

"You got that right." And she slams the door shut. Rolls her eyes. Says, "What a jerk."

"Um…" I peer at her carefully. "What just happened?"

She waves a hand dismissively. "He's just like the rest." Her grin is proud. "See? I'm finally learning the warning signs. I don't have time to waste on guys like that."

I don't know what to say. But she does. "What's with you and Kiara?"

"We had a fight."

"Hmm. Must have been a doozy." She kicks off her shoes and plops down on the couch. "Want to tell me about it?"

And I do. I tell her the whole stupid story. She doesn't say much until I'm done. Then she asks, "This all started over quizzes? And one of them had something to do with me?"

I hadn't meant to tell her that part, but it slipped out. In answer, I fetch my backpack and pull out my Sherry folder. She groans. "Not that thing. Didn't you see what I did with Clive? I don't need more lectures."

"This is something new. Just look at it." I hand her the questionnaire. "Please."

She sighs and rubs her forehead. "Fine." And then she starts reading. I watch her. Her eyebrows go up and down. Her lips purse. She frowns.

I take a bathroom break. When I get back, she's sitting with the questionnaire in her lap, gazing into midair.

"So," I say. "What do you think?"

She doesn't answer right away. Instead she asks, "What did you eat for dinner?"

I shrug. "Nothing."

"Me neither. What do you say we splurge and order in pizza?"

I know I should tell her we can't afford it. But I go get the takeout menu. Sherry calls in the order, then picks up the questionnaire. "This is interesting. It's about intimacy. Getting to know someone, right?"

I nod.

"I think *we* should do it. You and me."

"What? No." I shake my head. She can be so dense. "It's for you to do with guys you're dating."

"Yeah. But I think there are some questions here that we could ask each other.

Like this one. *How do you feel about your relationship with your mother?*"

I pick at a loose thread on the arm of the couch. I can't tell her the truth. As in, I don't have a "mother" relationship.

"Okay," she says. "Here's what I think. I think I'm a lousy mother. But the thing is, I don't know if I'll ever be able to act like a *proper* mother." Her smile is crooked. "It might have something to do with control issues. I've never been very good at controlling myself—never mind someone else."

"Are you saying Clive was right?" I ask. "You've got no discipline skills?"

She laughs. "No. I'm saying I don't know if that whole idea is right. Control for the sake of control doesn't work for me. Never has. I hated when my mother tried to run my life. Then again, if I'd listened to her, maybe my life would be different and…well, I'll just say it. I wouldn't have had you."

There it is. The plain, ugly truth. I came along and ruined her life. I can't look at her.

She leans toward me. "But there's another question here. It's about what we're grateful for. And Jane, I'm grateful for *you*. Okay? I know I suck at being a mom, but I hope you know I love you." Her voice cracks around a sob. "No matter what."

She's crying? She is. Her cheeks are wet with tears. And so are mine. I should say something. What comes out is, "Do you feel sorry for me?"

Her brows scrunch together. "What? No. Should I?"

I don't know why I said that. I shake my head. "No. Forget it. I meant, do you feel sorry for *you*? Yourself."

She snorts. "All the time."

"Because of me?"

She reaches out and grabs my hand. "Jane. What did I just tell you?

For someone so smart, you sure can be dense."

She thinks *I'm* dense? She goes on. "Listen. I feel sorry for myself because I have a crummy job, I don't have a man, I can't afford all the stuff I want." She pauses. "I really should do something about that, shouldn't I?"

"Yeah," I say. "You really need a rich new boyfriend, right?"

Sherry isn't listening. She's staring off into space again. "Maybe," she mutters, "I've been going about this the wrong way." She nods to herself. "Yeah. There was a time I planned to go to college. And how hard was it to kick Clive to the curb? Not hard at all. In fact, I sort of liked it."

"What are you saying?" I ask.

She looks at me. "I don't know for sure. I've got some thinking to do. But listen, when I said we were equals? I didn't mean you had to look after me instead of the other way around. I never wanted to put that on you."

"I don't—"

"Yes you do. You try to look after me. And that's sweet. I appreciate it. But what I said about me not liking to control or *be* controlled—that goes both ways." She grabs my hand again. "Jane. I want you to trust me to handle my life on my own terms, okay?"

"But…"

"Please," she says. "I need you to have some faith in me. No one else does. And I'll do the same for you. Like, this thing with Kiara? I know you'll work it out."

Tears gather in the back of my eyes, but I nod and blink them back. And then the door buzzer sounds, and Sherry goes to get the pizza. When she comes back, she finds a movie on TV for us to watch. Her favorite, a romantic comedy.

I tell myself nothing has changed. But I don't quite believe that.

Chapter Ten

The hours of the weekend inch by. If the hours were the pages in a book, they'd all be blank. I try to fill them. I work ahead on a report for social studies. It's about the Industrial Revolution, when the world turned gray. That's what it seems like— smoke and dust and steam rolling over lives. In my textbook's black-

and-white photos of that time, I see gray everywhere.

I pick a book to read from Neil deGrasse Tyson's list—*The Age of Reason*, by Thomas Paine. Tyson says it's on his list *to learn how the power of rational thought is the primary source of freedom in the world.* It sounds like something I need, and it's free online. But the book was published in 1794, and the language is old-school. It's a serious challenge to get through the first page. My brain rebels, and I give up.

I always thought I had a good brain. But it doesn't have any ideas on how to make me feel better. I consider my plans, my good, solid plans. They don't include guys. It dawns on me that they also don't include friends.

I guess I just assumed there would be friends. When I was younger, they were easy to find. But not anymore.

The only girl other than Kiara that I was ever close to moved away. Her flaky parents decided to go live on the land as hunter–gatherers. It all started with some sort of caveman diet they were on. It's impossible to keep in touch with someone living in a cave.

As for Kiara, we don't have much in common anymore. Maybe this fight is a good thing. I've outgrown her, right? I fill a whole blank-page hour by telling myself that. This is for the best. I'll join the chess club or volunteer for the school paper. I'll find smart, serious people to befriend. I don't know why I didn't realize this sooner. Friendships shouldn't happen by accident. There should be a selection process. Sherry was right about one thing. I will figure it out. I'll be in control of my life.

The last thing I do on Sunday night is check my phone for messages. There are none. Then I cry myself to sleep.

It's raining as I walk to school on Monday. It suits my mood perfectly. When it's time for Career and Personal Planning, I walk in with my armor on. Kiara isn't the only one who can be cold. I will not cast a single glance in her direction.

The work sheet on our desks today is quite short. It's about negative and positive behavior. All we have to do is list examples of each. Plenty of negative behaviors come to mind. Lying. Cheating. Holding grudges. Being fickle.

I could go on, but Ms. Kalkat interrupts. "Time for a class discussion."

In other words, a lecture. And, as usual, I'm right. She chatters away about positive behaviors. How hard work will pay off. How eating nutritious food keeps us healthy. Ditto for exercise and sleep.

And then she surprises us all by firing off a question. "What is self-respect?" Her sharp eyes roam our faces, and she picks on Lexi Taylor. "Lexi? Can you answer that, please?"

Lexi shifts in her seat and fiddles with her pen. "Um…I'd say it's sort of like self-esteem. Like, you feel that you're worth something."

Not bad.

Ms. Kalkat agrees. "Excellent answer. Self-respect means thinking well of yourself. And *caring* about yourself. One way we show ourselves that we care is to exercise self-control. And to not give that control to others." Once again her gaze wanders the room. "Liam. What is the danger of letting others control our behavior?"

He gawks at her. He obviously wasn't listening until he heard his name. "Huh?"

Ms. Kalkat walks toward him. She arches a brow and repeats the question.

"Okay," Liam says. "The danger of letting others control us." He's clearly stalling. "It's like, if you were asked a question that you didn't want to answer—then you wouldn't."

There are a few titters of laughter. Ms. Kalkat gives him the stare-down for a solid ten seconds. His grin fades. I'm dying to look at Kiara to see her reaction, but I resist. I wish Ms. Kalkat had asked me that question. I could give a good answer.

"You're not entirely wrong, Liam," Ms. Kalkat says. "But that's more an example than an answer. Anyone else?" She looks at us, waiting.

Before I can speak, Kiara says, "The danger in letting others control you is that you're not being true to yourself."

Wow. She knows that?

"Exactly." Ms. Kalkat nods.

Again, I have to force myself to *not* look at Kiara. Even though I feel that she is finally looking at me.

"All right, moving on." Ms. Kalkat steps back to the front of the room.

She rattles on again for a while. Stuff about setting boundaries in our relationships. I only half listen as I replay Kiara's answer in my head. There's something in it that makes my gut squirmy.

And then Ms. Kalkat surprises us again. "Staying with our theme, we can see that honesty is a positive behavior. How important is honesty in our relationships?"

Unbelievable. She's asking *that* question?

Her gaze falls on Javier. "Javier? Would you like to answer that?"

I clench my hands on the edges of my desk. I will *not* look at Kiara. I keep my eyes glued on Javier. I don't think I've ever heard him speak. Before he does, he bobs his head. And then, in a surprisingly deep voice, he says, "Honesty is very important in our relationships. Without honesty, there can be no trust."

A muffled shriek. I look up and lock eyes with Kiara. Her fist is pressed to her mouth, and she's bright pink. I feel heat rising in my own cheeks. I know what her astonished eyes are saying. *Omigod! It's him! He's the one!*

My eyes reply, *I know! Omigod! Who'd have thought?*

We need more than our eyes to discuss this. We need words. Many, many words. The air between us vibrates in anticipation of all that needs to be said. The bell to end class can't ring soon enough.

And then the elation in Kiara's face dies. If her face was a light, the dimmer switch would have moved from high to low—then turned completely off. She jerks her gaze from mine and hunches her shoulders. The wall of ice is back.

When I was small, I loved my grandpa's green glass ball. Even after he told me it was just an old fishing float, I thought it was magical. It was the size of a grapefruit, and the interior of that ball seemed full of promise. I was certain something was hidden inside. Not only that, but it had floated on the ocean. Where had it been? What stories might it tell? I would peer into its green depths and wonder. One day I dropped it, and the glass float shattered into dull fragments of nothing. Garbage to be swept up and thrown away.

I feel like that now. For a moment I was filled with green promise, able to float. To go far. And now I'm nothing more than scattered splinters.

Chapter Eleven

The rest of the day seems to last forever. I want nothing more than to hide from the world. Being surrounded by a sea of people who don't see me is lonelier than being alone. At one point, I pass by Javier in the hall. He bobs his head. I bob mine. And that's all. I wonder how many of us float past each other, people with depths no one sees. I wonder if

I'm right to shun all boys just because they're male.

Mostly, I wonder about what Kiara said. *The danger in letting others control you is that you're not being true to yourself.* Does she realize how controlling she's been? And why does all this stuff about control keep coming up? First with Sherry, and now this.

I'm still thinking about it as I walk home. I remember a quiz Kiara did. It had something to do with attraction. Discover the best color to attract things you want from the universe? It was as hokey as all the others. She was really excited to learn she should surround herself with purple. For about a week, she wore purple. Her top or ponytail band or socks or *something* would be purple. She claimed it worked because she got what she wanted. Her cheerleading squad chose to do the routine she liked best.

I figured it was a fluke. But if there *is* something to it, maybe we can also attract things we *don't* want. Like, me hearing about control all over the place? I don't want to hear any more about it. Why?

Because...

Because control is trickier than the coyote. I thought it was about taking charge of my life. I started with my ten-year plan. The world was chaotic with Sherry, and I needed order. But somehow that turned into trying to control Sherry?

And then Kiara. She's always held the power in our friendship. Even when we met, in second grade, she called the shots. And I was fine with it until... I wasn't. But instead of simply standing up for myself, I became her. A controller.

I let myself into our apartment and sag against the door. It's true. I told myself I was helping them, but was I?

Would I want them teaching me lessons? Telling me they know better? Trying to stop me from being who I am? No. Well, maybe if I was about to do something nasty or dangerous. Like hurt myself or someone else. It isn't easy to find the line between caring and controlling. But at least I've noticed there is a line.

I expel a huge breath, and the clench in my gut eases— it's relieved I finally figured it out. Maybe there is something to those gut instincts people talk about. Like using your instincts on a quiz to choose between a grassy meadow, a beach and a full moon.

Bad example. But thinking about Kiara's quizzes again has given me an idea. A great idea! Or not? Some of my recent great ideas didn't turn out so well.

Still, the more I think about it, the more hopeful I am. It might work. I've got nothing to lose by trying. I go to the computer and do a search for a free online quiz-building site. I find one that's easy to use, and start typing. It's like working on the toughest school assignment ever. And the most important one. Yet my fingers fly over the keyboard, barely able to keep up with my thoughts.

When I'm done, I read over what I've written. It's a quiz especially for Kiara. A friendship quiz. It won't pop up an answer for her, but I hope it provides an answer all the same. I want to give it to her right away. Since she blocked me, I can't send it online. It would be awkward to go to her house. I decide to send it in a text message. Before I can second-guess myself, it's done. The link is attached to a blank message, and boom. It's sent.

Now? Now I wait. I notice my heart is beating a little too fast. I stand up and prowl around the apartment. It feels like a cage. Maybe I should have printed the quiz and taken it to her? I return to the computer and press *Print*.

But no, I can't do that. Instead, I pick up a pen and answer the quiz myself. All it takes is a flurry of check marks. I stare at my completed quiz for a full minute. Then I take a picture of it and send that to Kiara too. I can't expect her to answer it without doing it myself. If nothing else, at least it will show her how I feel.

Friendship Quiz

You and your friend have a disagreement. You: (Check all that apply)

A. Tell her she's an idiot.
B. Argue with her until she gives in (even though she might resent you).
C. Get someone else to take your side against her.
D. Try to understand her point of view. ✓

Your friend has changed. She isn't the same person she used to be. You:

  A. Ditch her.
  B. Slowly drift away and become distant.
  C. Accept her changes. ✓
  D. Tell her to go back to how she was before.

Which signs tell you to keep your friend?

  A. Your differences make the friendship interesting. ✓
  B. You love talking with her and figuring out the world. ✓
  C. She knows you're not perfect. ✓
  D. You have fun and feel safe with her. ✓

If you decide to make up with your friend, you:

  A. Forgive her and put the past behind you. ✓
  B. Hold out for a while to teach her a lesson.

C. Think about what you need to say to her. ✓
D. Call her right away. ✓

My phone rings.

Chapter Twelve

I answer the call on the first ring. It's Sherry. "Hey," she says. "How's it going?"

I croak, "Fine."

"Don't give me *fine*. Did you and Kiara make up?"

I bite down on my lip. "Not yet."

Her sigh comes through the phone. "I'm sorry to hear that. I was calling to say I'll be late coming home."

I won't ask. I don't want to hear about
the latest loser. I want to crawl into bed
and hide under the covers. I say, "Okay."

"Don't you want to know why?" she
asks.

"Whatever."

There's another sigh. "It's not what
you think. I'm going to swing by the
college."

The college? "What?"

She laughs. "I know. Weird, eh? It's
just to get some information. You know,
a look-see."

"You're going to scope out the
professors?"

"Jane. Please. I'm going to check
out some courses."

My mind boggles. "You're going
back to school?"

"I don't know for sure. Maybe."

"Wow."

"I know." She clears her throat. "I'm
sort of nervous."

"That's great," I say.

"It's great that I'm nervous?"

"No." I laugh. "That you're going to check it out."

"You think?" She pauses. "Then again, you've given me an idea."

"I have?"

"Yeah," she says. "If the courses don't look possible, maybe the professors…"

"Sherry. No. Be true to yourself." I can't believe I said that to her.

Sherry laughs. "Now I'm confused. If I'm true to myself, the professors *will* be my focus."

"Not if you are true to the person you *really* are."

There's a stretch of silence before she replies. "When did you get to be so smart?"

"I was born this way."

"You were," she says. "I've never been able to figure out how that happened."

"I got it from you. College mom."

"Aw. Thanks, Jane. See you later?"

"Yeah."

We hang up, and I sit with the phone in my hand, thinking. People do change. They really do. And sometimes that's a good thing. Other times…

My phone rings again. It startles me so much, I drop it. Then I fumble to pick it up and answer. The display says it's Kiara. My hands are instantly sweaty, and I accidentally disconnect the call. I immediately call her back. Her line is busy. I try again. Still busy. I leave her a voice message. "Hey. Sorry. Call me back."

Then my phone shows I have a message. I call in to my voice mail, and hear Kiara's message: "You hung up on me?"

Oh man. We've done this before. If I try calling her back again now, she could be calling me. It could go on forever.

Or for at least ten minutes, like the other time we got tangled up in this loop. I can't take it. I throw on my jacket and bolt.

I run all the way to her house. By the time I get there, all of me is sweaty. And then I lose my nerve. I don't know what she wanted to say. What if it isn't what I hope to hear? I edge into the front yard. Then I duck behind a shrub to catch my breath. Also to hide.

I decide to check my phone for further messages, and suddenly the shrub starts rustling. It's really moving. I freeze and gawk at it for a second. But when I turn to flee, something grabs my ankle. And another something grabs my arm. I scream.

And then I realize it's only the twins. They release me and roll about on the grass, laughing like maniacs. In unison they crow, "We got you, Jane!"

"Yeah," I say sourly. "You did."

"You didn't even see us playing spy. We got you good."

"Yeah yeah." I glare at them, but it's hard to keep the glare. "Little brats." I've missed them. So much. I cross my arms over my stomach and turn to leave.

"Hey! Where are you going?"

"Yeah. You just got here. You can't go yet." They leap up and grab hold of my jacket. Then they start yelling, "Kiara! Kiara! Jane's here. We've got her!"

Could this get any more embarrassing? I try to shake them off, but they're tough little fiends. I may have to give up my jacket and make a run for it. They're not allowed past the stop sign on the corner, so if I can sprint that far…

Instead, I trip and tumble to the grass. Things get rapidly worse. They sit on me. And keep yelling. "Kiara! Kiara!"

She finds us like that.

Chapter Thirteen

A decent friend would scold the boys and pull them off. Does Kiara do that? No. She slaps a hand to her mouth, but that does nothing to hide her laughter. Pretty soon she's bent double and gasping. Finally, she collapses beside us. "Boys. Let go of Jane."

"Aw, do we have to?"

"Is she going to leave?"

Kiara looks at me directly. "I hope not."

My glasses were already crooked. Now the tears springing to my eyes make them fog up.

Kiara tells the twins, "Mom has ice cream." And they're gone.

I take a moment to sit up and brush myself off. To remove my glasses and clean them. To take a steadying breath before I say, "Thanks for rescuing me."

She grins. "Anytime." Then her smile wavers. "So," she says. "I got your quiz."

I nod. "And…did you like it?"

She bends her head and starts plucking at the grass. I wait. Finally she says softly, "I'm sorry, Jane."

I blink. "You're sorry? No, *I'm* sorry." Then an awful thought occurs to me. "Unless—are you saying you *didn't* like the quiz?"

She swats my arm. "Of course I liked it! I *loved* it. Man, for someone so smart, you sure can be—"

"I know. Dense."

"Yeah. But I can be too. I was just so angry." She shakes her head. "And hurt."

"I'm sorry," I repeat. "I get it. Really."

Her lip starts trembling. "I felt like you betrayed me. And I couldn't even *tell* anyone about it. Because then I'd have to tell them about the fake quiz. And it was all so…" She waves a hand in the air.

"Wacky?" I suggest.

"Exactly. And it was so *us*. No one else would get it."

This is true. "It was *your* idea."

"Yeah. But you went along with it. To a point." She eyes me. "It was *your* idea to convince the other kids in fourth grade that we were witches."

"Because of that wart I had."

She wrinkles her nose. "That wart was freakin' weird."

I shrug. "It worked. They stopped bugging me about it. But if we're bringing up old scams, what about sixth grade? *You* photoshopped us into those African safari pictures."

"That was good, wasn't it?" She grins. "Lexi still asks me about that trip. She really wants to go one day."

"I hope she does. She'll just have to plan for it." Plan. I like plans. But thinking about that reminds me about the flaws in mine. It reminds me of something else too. I look at Kiara carefully. "Kiara? I really *am* sorry. I shouldn't have interfered with your plan. I can't expect you to be like me."

"No," she sighs, "you can't. Although in some ways I wish I could be more like you."

This is surprising. "You do? Then why did you say…" I can't say it.

111

"What? What did I say?" And then she flushes pink and looks away. "Oh. That. I said I felt sorry for you." She grabs the end of her ponytail and starts twisting it. "I didn't really mean it."

"But there must be something to it. Is it because I'm such a nerd? Or because I'm almost poor? Or"—I hesitate—"because of Sherry?"

She nods. "Because of Sherry."

"Actually, she's thinking about going—" I begin.

"Wait." Kiara cuts in. "I should explain. It's not because Sherry is such a flake. I mean, maybe she can't help it. She just *is* one. And I get that that sucks for you. But the reason I felt sorry was more because you let her affect you too much."

I do? "What do you mean?"

Kiara looks at me intently. "I know she's not the ideal mom. But she cares about you. In her way. And I'm not saying it's okay that she is how she is. It's just I think *you'd* be happier if you could accept her for who she is."

"So you're saying I shouldn't try to fix her?"

Kiara nods. "Yeah. You are so worried about her and about not *being* her that you don't get to be *you*."

It's possible that Kiara understands me better than I understand myself. "So...who am I?"

She raises an eyebrow. "You're asking me?"

I grimace. "Not really. I know I need to figure it out for myself. And...stand up for myself."

"Yeah." She sighs again. "You do. I get that. And I know I can be sort of bossy sometimes. I just wish you hadn't decided to stand up for yourself when you did." Before I can reply, she adds, "But then, if you *hadn't*, I might never have known about Javier."

Her mom yells from the door. "Girls. Hurry up. Supper's on the table. It's getting cold."

Kiara rolls her eyes. "Talk about bossy. I think I inherited it."

I remember my weird reaction to body contact with Liam and shudder. "Please don't tell me we're all about heredity."

She grins. "I doubt it. So are you staying? You have to stay. My mom's been after me all week to make up with you. And besides, I need to talk to you about Javier."

Chapter Fourteen

I'm really glad some things don't have to change. Chiles rellenos for one. Hanging out with my bestie for two. Sinking into the chair in Kiara's room after supper feels like being tucked in. Like getting an A on an essay. Like finding red hair in the bathroom. Comfortable. Right.

I tell Kiara about Sherry's new school interest, and she's delighted.

I send Sherry a text to tell her where I am. She replies, **Awesome! I knew you'd work it out. The college is huge. I got lost, and this really hot guy helped me out. Later!**

I show the text to Kiara. We laugh. And then she takes over. A week of missed conversation pours forth. Most of it centers on Javier.

"His answers to our quiz were very cool."

"True." They were.

"And I did this new online quiz, right?"

"Of course you did," I reply.

"It was about finding your soul connections."

Oh man.

"But guess what?" Her eyes are round. "That's not the same thing as a soul mate."

"Really?"

She nods. "Soul connections can happen all over the place. With food, places, friends, animals…the list goes on. So here's what I'm thinking. I don't find Javier attractive."

"No?"

She shakes her head. "No. He's not my type."

"Your type is more like Liam?"

She wrinkles her nose. "Not. He's way too into himself. I have coyote spirit wisdom, right? I can't be tricked by appearances."

How could I ever have thought about giving up this friendship?

"So forget about him," Kiara says. "But Javier. He's interesting. And smart. Don't you think?"

I nod. I do.

"So I'd like to get to know him better. And I was thinking I might…"

"Give him another quiz?" I ask.

She frowns. "I thought about it. But I decided I just want to talk to him. Maybe be his friend. In case he's a soul connection."

I'm not ready to share Kiara with someone else yet. An uncomfortable jealousy rises up in me. I swallow it down. "Oh?"

"Yeah. And I think you'd like him too. Or he'd like you."

"But—"

She holds up a hand. "I know. Guys aren't in *the plan*. I get it. But Jane, that is so racist."

I gape at her. "*Racist?* Ugh. Kiara…"

"Ha. I knew that would get a reaction. I *know* it's not racist, okay? I mean, obviously. But it's sort of like that. You won't associate with guys just because they're guys."

Should I admit that I've already had doubts about that part of my plan? "Yes, but—"

"No buts! All I'm saying is, who doesn't want to be friends with someone who wants to invent a time machine? Or whose perfect day is go on safari and feast and sleep under the stars?"

"Or whose future plans are to follow their curiosity?" I mutter. That boggles my mind. Because it doesn't really sound like a plan. Except it is.

"Yeah! I think that might be my plan too. So here's what I want to do."

She tells me. I listen. And I decide I'm good with it. The next day at lunch, we ambush Javier in the hall. We walk up to him with a book we got from the library—*The Time Machine* by H.G. Wells. We ask him if he's read it. We haven't read it, but he has. And it's like turning on a tap. Javier talks. And talks. About time travel. Where and when he'd like to go. About how changing one little thing can have ripple effects. About how hard it would be to be stuck in a place and time where you don't know anyone. How unpredictable the future is.

I'm fascinated. I could listen to him for hours. I love the way he waves his hands around to make a point. His curly hair vibrates, and I want to touch it. His eyes shine with delight. But when I glance at Kiara to share my wonder, I notice that her eyes have glazed over. I nudge her with my elbow, and she starts. She looks around like she's searching for the exit and spots Lexi coming down the hall. Then she blurts, "So, Javier. What do you think about traveling to the African savanna?"

His eyes widen. His head bobs. He starts talking about a goat-grazing project on the grasslands. Kiara looks horrified.

I'm amazed at how informed he is. I slip in a question. "So the goats actually improved the grasslands?"

Javier turns to me. "Yes. But the grazing must be rotated." He begins describing how the farmers manage this. I listen.

It takes me a moment to notice Kiara has run away. I'm forced to make a decision. I hold up a hand. "Javier?"

He stops.

"Can we talk about this again sometime?"

He nods. And smiles. He has a wonderful smile. I probably smile too—I'm not sure. And then I go after Kiara. When I catch up to her, she's sulky.

"What's wrong?" I ask.

"You were right. Guys are a waste of time."

"Not all of them," I protest. "Javier's incredibly smart."

"Yeah. Maybe *too* smart. And he talks too much." She catches my eye and shakes her head. "Don't even, Jane.

I know, okay? I do it too. But obviously, there can only be *one* motormouth on the scene. Two together is a tragedy."

"You have a point. But maybe he's lonely. Maybe he had a lot bottled up because no one ever talks to him. Or no one lets *him* talk."

Kiara considers this. "That would be awful."

"I know."

"So maybe…" She pauses and twists her ponytail. "Maybe I'll have to share you."

I raise my brows. "Share me?"

"Yeah. Like, when I'm at cheerleading? Or if I ever do find the one? You could hang out with Javier."

"Really?" I can't keep the sarcasm from my tone. "You'd *allow* that?"

She looks at me sideways. "It's not like that." She reads my eyes. "No? Okay. You're right. I guess you need to do whatever you want."

I sigh. "I guess we both do. The thing is, Kiara…" I stop. Start again. "The thing is, you're my bestie. Forever, I hope. But I have a feeling we're going to keep changing. And there will be times when it can't be just us. So I like your idea."

She squints at me. "Which one?"

"I *would* like to hang out with Javier."

Her squint narrows. Her eyes are mere slits. "You'd like that?"

"I think he's interesting and actually sort of…cute."

Kiara gapes at me. Then she cranes her neck to peer down the hall at Javier. "Seriously?"

I shrug.

She grins and links her arm through mine. "But I'll still be your bestie?"

"Always."

She smiles. "Okay then."

I nod. And it is okay. All of it.

ACKNOWLEDGMENTS

Gratitude to my wise friends, Diane Tullson and Shelley Hrdlitschka, ever there to quiz me on my writing. And many thanks again to Melanie Jeffs, editor, and the talented team at Orca Book Publishers.

K.L. Denman has written many novels for youth, including the Orca Currents titles *Destination Human* and *Agent Angus*. She lives in Delta, British Columbia. For more information, visit www.kldenman.com.